MIRIAM YOUNG

IF I RODE A DINOSAUR

ILLUSTRATED BY ROBERT QUACKENBUSH

LOTHROP, LEE & SHEPARD CO. / NEW YORK

ISBN 0-688-41591-1   ISBN 0-688-51591-6 (lib. bdg.)   1 2 3 4 5 78 77 76 75 74

I think that giant dinosaurs would be such fun to ride,
If only I could figure out a way to get astride.

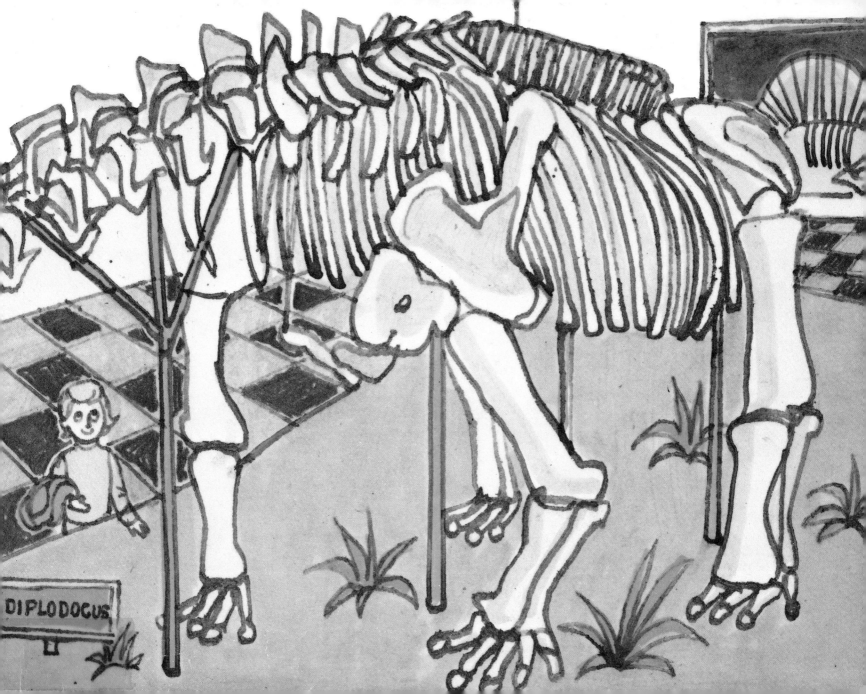

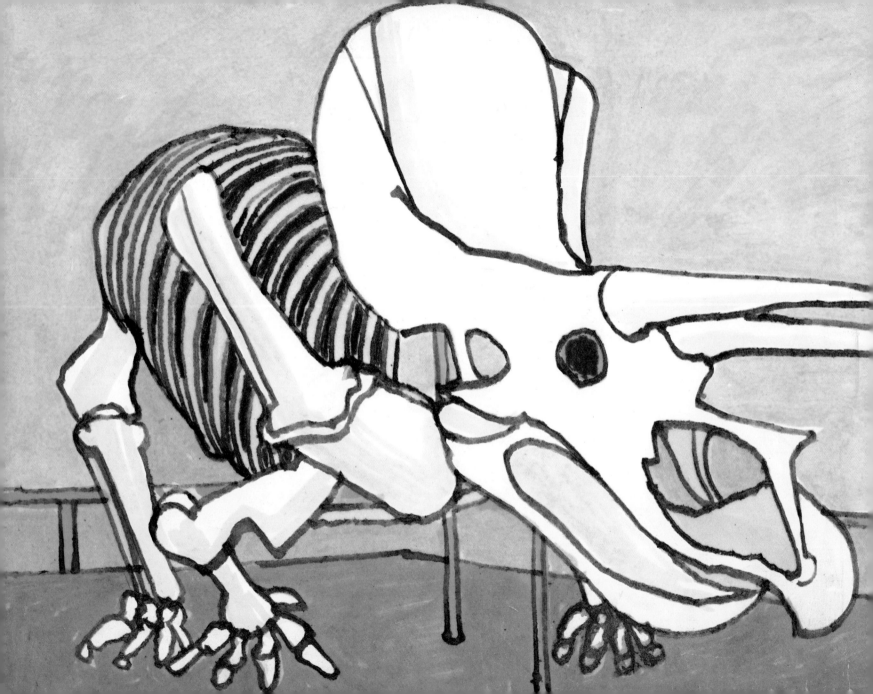

When I go to the Museum of Natural History, I like to look at the skeletons of those monsters who lived millions of years ago. I keep thinking how great it would be if they were around now. I'd tame them and train them to carry me around on their backs. It might be a little scary but it certainly would be fun.

TRICERATOPS

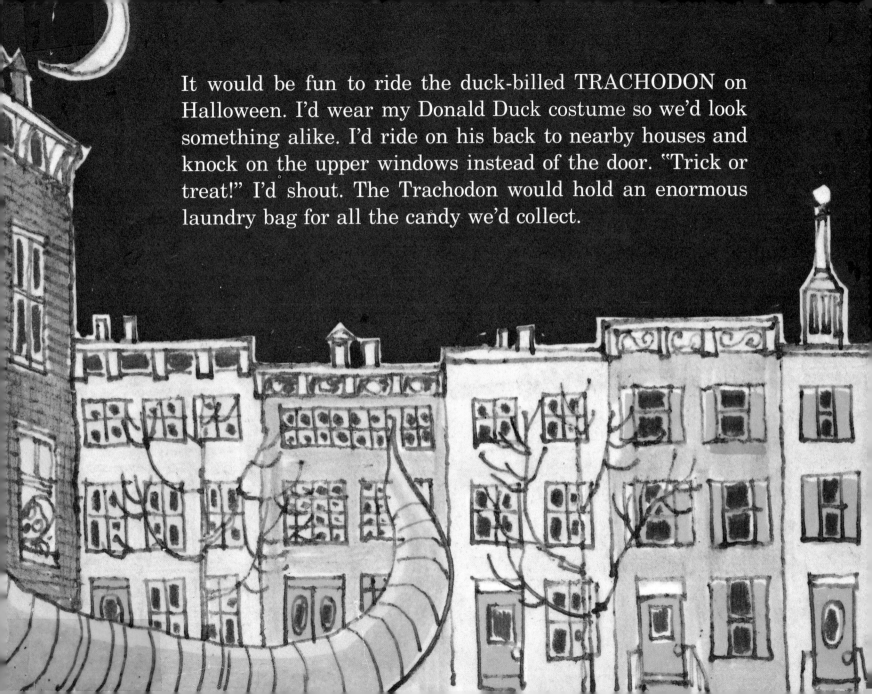

It would be fun to ride the duck-billed TRACHODON on Halloween. I'd wear my Donald Duck costume so we'd look something alike. I'd ride on his back to nearby houses and knock on the upper windows instead of the door. "Trick or treat!" I'd shout. The Trachodon would hold an enormous laundry bag for all the candy we'd collect.

If I could ride a DIPLODOCUS—the longest dinosaur, as long as three school buses—I'd ride him to the middle of the river and stop. His head would reach one bank, his tail the other. He'd keep busy nibbling water plants all day and I'd set up a tollbooth for people who wanted a short cut across the river. A sign would say, "STOP AND PAY TOLL. ONE LOLLIPOP (NO PURPLE)." Red is my favorite flavor. And at supper time I'd ride him home again.

If I could ride a MONOCLONIUS—a large one-horned dinosaur—I'd take him to birthday parties and we could play ring-toss on his horn. That kind of dinosaur eats only vegetables, so we wouldn't offer him any ice cream or cake. But I'd take him home to supper and let him eat my broccoli or spinach or lima beans.

It would be neat to ride a PTERANODON, who looks like a giant bat. I'd fly to school and do the loop-the-loop over the school buildings. The children would dash to the windows, and the teachers, too. We'd glide and soar and swoop over the playground, and I'd drop leaflets to the teachers from my mother: "Please excuse my child from school this week. The Pteranodon needs exercise."

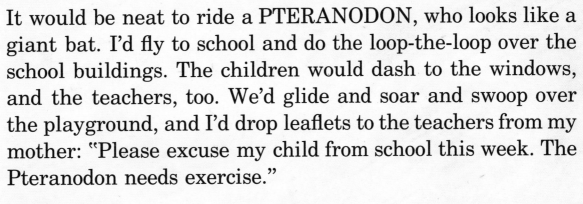

It would be fun to ride the ELASMOSAURUS, a long-necked sea serpent with a turtle-like body and long flippers. I'd take him to the beach when we went on vacation. I'd ride along on his back as he swam around catching fish. It would be like riding a swan-boat with an automatic fishing pole! He'd catch enough for himself and us, and we'd cook ours on the beach.

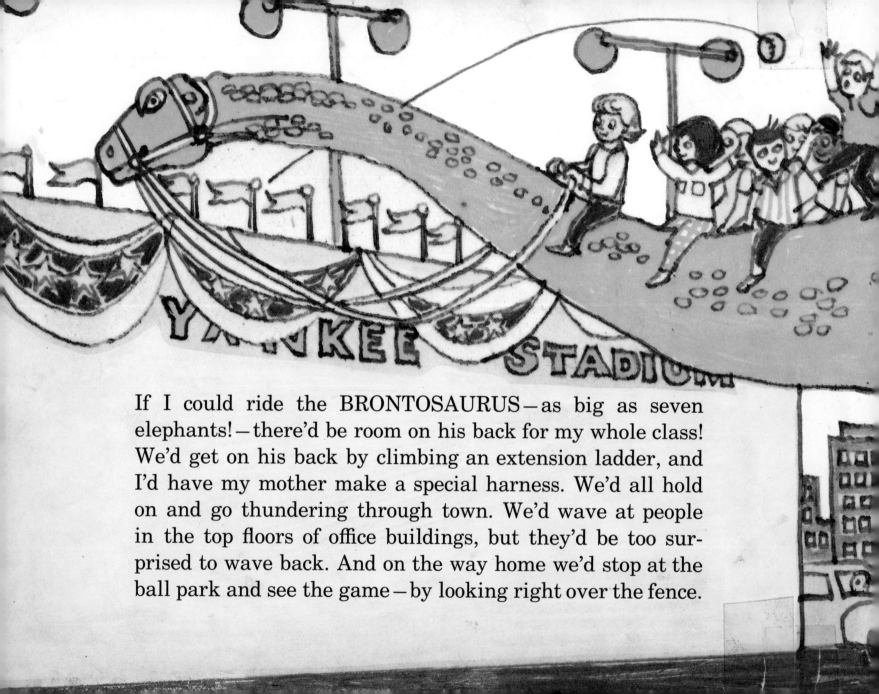

If I could ride the BRONTOSAURUS—as big as seven elephants!—there'd be room on his back for my whole class! We'd get on his back by climbing an extension ladder, and I'd have my mother make a special harness. We'd all hold on and go thundering through town. We'd wave at people in the top floors of office buildings, but they'd be too surprised to wave back. And on the way home we'd stop at the ball park and see the game—by looking right over the fence.

But the Brontosaurus is so big and heavy, he'd just plod along. So maybe I'd rather ride an ORNITHOMIMUS because it's a fast runner. It looks like an ostrich, but has arms instead of wings and a long tail instead of feathers. It would be great to ride at football practice. My friend Kenny would throw the ball and I'd go dashing down the field on my Ornithomimus. It has long grasping fingers—just perfect for making the catch.

A STYRACOSAURUS would be handy to take on camping trips, and more fun to ride than a bike. I wouldn't have to pack anything. My knapsack, my canteen, my cap, and everything else could just be hooked on his horns. When we got home I'd ride him along our hedge and he'd clip it for my father with his strong beak. He'd be glad to do it, because to him it would be like me eating Rice Krispies or potato chips —just nice and crunchy.

It would be terrific to have a CAMPTOSAURUS to ride in summer. My friends and I could take turns sliding down his back. I'd tie him up near the wading pool, and while he was nibbling leaves from a nearby tree, we'd go sliding down into the water—splash! He wouldn't mind, I'm sure. It ought to feel like having your back rubbed.

I'd like to ride
a BRACHIOSAURUS
when we went to the beach. I'd get
up early and sneak him into the water, when
no one was looking. He has an extra nostril in a dome on top
of his head, so he can submerge all the way with just that
nostril sticking out to breathe through. So when I rode on
his back, all anybody would see was me! They'd see me skim-
ming along and think, "Wow! What a fast swimmer!" Or
they'd see me sitting there, as if I were sitting on the water,
and they'd think I must be magic.

Another sea serpent I'd like to ride is the TYLOSAURUS, as big as a whale. I'd keep it in the lake at Grandma's. Most of the time he'd swim underwater. Then suddenly he'd appear—and disappear again. The newspapers would report, "Monster sighted in local lake. Real or imaginary?" Then one day I'd swim out and get on his back and ride him in to shore. Everyone would rush to take our picture. And we'd appear on the evening news on TV.

If I had a TRICERATOPS to ride, it would be like having my own private dragon. I'd ride along, sitting just back of his head, and his big bony frill would act like a windshield. He'd be great to take on snowball fights in winter. When a snowball came at me, I could just duck down and never get hit. And I could train him to catch snowballs on his horns.

And then there's TYRANNOSAURUS REX, the most ferocious animal who ever lived, with a jaw as big as a steam shovel and teeth like daggers. If I rode Tyrannosaurus Rex, I'd take him to the dentist's and pretend he had a toothache. "Be careful, Dentist," I would say. "He may be feeling fierce today. And when you tell him, 'Open wide,' you might just disappear inside."

I'm sure I'd have a lot of fun
With all these monsters, every one.
Too bad they're not here any more,
I'd *love* to ride a dinosaur.